YASMIN

The Writer

written by
SAADIA FARUQI

illustrated by
HATEM ALY

PICTURE WINDOW BOOKS
a capstone imprint

To Mariam for inspiring me, and Mubashir
for helping me find the right words—S.F.

To my sister, Eman, and her amazing girls,
Jana and Kenzi—H.A.

Yasmin is published by Picture Window Books, an imprint of Capstone.
1710 Roe Crest Drive
North Mankato, Minnesota 56003
www.capstonepub.com

Text copyright © 2020 by Saadia Faruqi.
Illustrations copyright © 2020 by Picture Window Books.

Library of Congress Cataloging-in-Publication Data
Names: Faruqi, Saadia, author. | Aly, Hatem, illustrator.
Title: Yasmin the writer / written by Saadia Faruqi ; illustrated by
Hatem Aly.
Description: [North Mankato : Picture Window Books, 2020] | Series:
Yasmin | Audience: Ages 5-8. | Audience: Grades K-1. | Summary:
Yasmin struggles with Ms. Alex's assignment to write an essay about
her hero until she realizes that her hero is someone very close to her.
Identifiers: LCCN 2019047860 (print) | LCCN 2019047861 (ebook) |
ISBN 9781515846437 (hardcover) | ISBN 9781515858874 (paperback) |
ISBN 9781515846482 (pdf)
Subjects: CYAC: Heroes--Fiction. | Creative writing--Fiction. | Schools-
-Fiction. | Mothers and daughters--Fiction. | Pakistani Americans--
Fiction. | Muslims--United States--Fiction.
Classification: LCC PZ7.1.F373 Yn 2020 (print) | LCC PZ7.1.F373
(ebook) | DDC [E]--dc23
LC record available at https://lccn.loc.gov/2019047860
LC ebook record available at https://lccn.loc.gov/2019047861

Editorial Credits:
Kristen Mohn, editor; Lori Bye and Kay Fraser, designers; Jo Miller,
media researcher; Tori Abraham, production specialist

Design Elements:
Shutterstock: Art and Fashion, rangsan paidaen

TABLE OF CONTENTS

CHAPTER 1

The Assignment

Ms. Alex had a new assignment for the students. "You're each going to write an essay!" she said.

Yasmin raised her hand. "I like writing!" she said. "What will we write about?"

Ms. Alex wrote the topic on the board. **My Hero**. "Does anyone know what a hero is?" she asked.

Emma raised her hand. "Someone who does great things. Someone we can be proud of," she said.

Ms. Alex nodded. "Absolutely!"

Ali was too excited to wait for Ms. Alex to call on him.

"I will write about Muhammad Ali, the boxing champ," he said. "We have the same name. He's my hero!"

"Great choice," Ms. Alex said
with a smile.

"I think I'll write about Rosa
Parks," Emma said. "She was a
brave hero!"

Yasmin tapped her pencil.
Who should she write her essay
about? She couldn't come up
with any heroes.

The bell rang.

"Work on a rough draft tonight," Ms. Alex said. "We'll write our essays tomorrow after lunch."

CHAPTER 2

Thinking Hard

That evening Mama showed Yasmin how to research on the computer while dinner was cooking.

"Here is a list of people who have done amazing things," Mama said.

On the list were a famous

athlete and a music star. There

was a man who donated lots

of money to poor people. There

were queens, presidents, and

other leaders.

But Yasmin shook her head.
"None of these are *my* heroes."

"Keep thinking while I
finish making dinner," Mama
said. "Look, we're having your
favorite—keema!"

Yasmin doodled on her paper.

"Thanks," she mumbled. Writing

an essay wasn't as easy as she'd

thought.

The phone rang.

"I got it!" Mama yelled.

Yasmin made a list of ideas.

An explorer? An inventor? A

poet? She sighed and crossed

them out. These were amazing

people. But who was her hero?

"Mama, I can't find my pajamas," Yasmin said at bedtime.

Mama found them in the closet. "Here they are, jaan!"

That night Yasmin had a
bad dream. She woke up scared.
Mama came into her room and
held her close.

"It's okay, my darling," Mama
said softly. "You're safe. I'm
always here."

CHAPTER 3

A Hero to the Rescue

The next morning at school, the students showed their homework. Emma's rough draft had facts about Rosa Parks.

Ali had drawn a picture of Muhammad Ali with his boxing gloves.

Yasmin shoved her blank

paper into her desk.

At lunch she realized she'd

forgotten her lunch box. "Oh

no!" she wailed. Her day was

getting worse and worse.

Suddenly Mama burst into the cafeteria.

"Yasmin! I'm here!" she panted. She held up Yasmin's lunch box.

"Mama, you're a lifesaver!"

Yasmin said and hugged her.

Mama hugged Yasmin back.

"That's just what mothers do."

Yasmin got an idea. "I guess you could say you're my hero!"

After lunch Yasmin knew exactly who to write about.

My hero is my Mama. She juggles many different jobs at home like an expert. She hugs me when I'm worried or sad. She protects me. She saves me from an empty stomach. She is always there. I don't know what I'd do without Mama.

Ms. Alex peeked over Yasmin's shoulder. "Excellent essay, Yasmin! Heroes don't have to be famous people. Sometimes they are the ones closest to us."

Think About It, Talk About It

* Yasmin can't think of an idea to write about—she has writer's block! When you have trouble coming up with an idea, how do you find inspiration?

* Who is your hero? Write three sentences that tell why this person is important to you.

* Look at the pictures in the story. How do the pictures show Mama being a hero to Yasmin?

Learn Urdu with Yasmin!

Yasmin's family speaks both English and Urdu. Urdu is a language from Pakistan. Maybe you already know some Urdu words!

baba (BAH-bah)—father

hijab (HEE-jahb)—scarf covering the hair

jaan (jahn)—life; a sweet nickname for a loved one

kameez (kuh-MEEZ)—long tunic or shirt

keema (KEE-mah)—ground meat dish

mama (MAH-mah)—mother

nana (NAH-nah)—grandfather on mother's side

nani (NAH-nee)—grandmother on mother's side

salaam (sah-LAHM)—hello

shukriya (shuh-KREE-yuh)—thank you

Pakistani Fun Facts

Yasmin and her family are proud of their Pakistani culture. Yasmin loves to share facts about Pakistan!

Location

Pakistan is on the continent of Asia, with India on one side and Afghanistan on the other.

Islamabad

PAKISTAN

Population

Pakistan's population is more than 200,000,000 people. It is the world's sixth-most-populous country.

Culture

A famous, award-winning Pakistani writer in the U.S. is Bapsi Sidhwa.

The word *Pakistan* means "land of the pure" in Urdu and Persian.

The first Pakistani to have traveled to the North and South Poles is a young woman named Namira Salim.

Make Your Own Writing Journal

SUPPLIES:

- cereal box or other thin cardboard
- scissors
- about 10 sheets of paper
- hole punch
- yarn
- markers

STEPS:

1. Cut a rectangular piece of cardboard twice as big as you'd like your journal to be.

2. Hold the shorter sides of the rectangle and fold it in half. If the cardboard has a picture you don't want to show, fold so that the plain side faces out.

3. Cut the papers so they're just a bit smaller than the cardboard covers. Stack the papers inside the cardboard like the pages of a book.

4. Along the cardboard fold, use the hole punch to make two punches, evenly spaced. Make sure you punch down through the papers too.

5. Thread a piece of yarn through each hole and tie a knot to hold your pages in place.

6. Draw a design on the front of your journal!

About the Author

Saadia Faruqi is a Pakistani American writer, interfaith activist, and cultural sensitivity trainer previously profiled in *O Magazine*. She is editor-in-chief of *Blue Minaret*, a magazine for Muslim art, poetry, and prose. Saadia is also author of the adult short story collection, *Brick Walls: Tales of Hope & Courage from Pakistan*. Her essays have been published in *Huffington Post*, *Upworthy*, and *NBC Asian America*. She resides in Houston, Texas, with her husband and children.

Hatem Aly is an Egyptian-born illustrator whose work has been featured in multiple publications worldwide. He currently lives in beautiful New Brunswick, Canada, with his wife, son, and more pets than people. When he is not dipping cookies in a cup of tea or staring at blank pieces of paper, he is usually drawing books. One of the books he illustrated is *The Inquisitor's Tale* by Adam Gidwitz, which won a Newbery Honor and other awards, despite Hatem's drawings of a farting dragon, a two-headed cat, and stinky cheese.

Join Yasmin
on all her adventures!

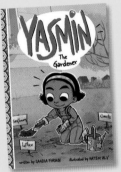

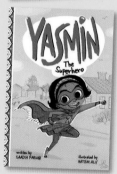

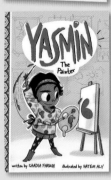